Ninja Kids

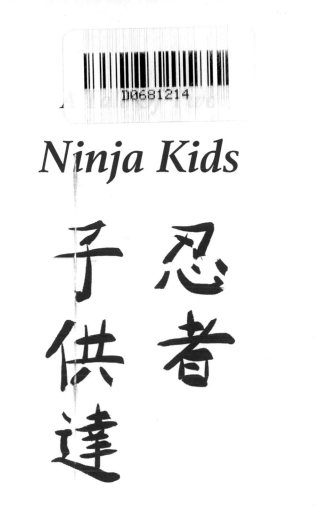

Book 1

A Martial Arts Adventure Story

By Adam Oakley

COPYRIGHT

ISBN: 9781973495932

www.AdamOakleyBooks.com

www.InnerPeaceNow.com

Published by Oakhouse Publications.

Oakhouse Publications

Contents

Welcome

Nunchuks

Throwing Darts

若武者

Throwing Stars

Daggers

Young Warrior

Ninja Swords

Chapter 1 - Ninja Kids

There were two young ninjas who lived on opposite sides of the world.

One was a young boy living in Japan, who had been born into a family of ninjas. His name was Myasako. He always wanted to be like one of the normal boys, able to relax and play and laugh and have fun after school. His was a life of hard work and discipline. He was trained to be a killer, an assassin that could move silently, and for those kinds of skills to be developed, his father expected nothing but total commitment from his son.

The other ninja was a young boy who lived in England. His name was Martin.

Martin was a boy who was able to have fun and laugh and play with his friends after school, but he always wanted the life of a ninja. He always wanted to be trained by a ninja, to move silently and use his body as a weapon. He wanted to learn how to use other weapons as well – nunchuks, daggers, throwing darts – everything that a ninja would be able to use.

Each boy wanted the other one's life, but they had never met before.

"Father. I wish to be away from all of this," the young Japanese boy said. "You work me too hard.

My entire life is work, training, always trying to be faster and stronger and more accurate with my skills. You never allow me any rest."

His father stared down at the young boy in front of him.

"Excellence is a full-time occupation," his father said. "There is no time off for the excellent. Look at how fast, how flexible, how strong you have become already. If anyone was to challenge you, you could defend yourself with ease. Your timing, your speed, your…"

"But you won't even let me go outside and play! Who am I supposed to be defending myself from if I don't have any life in the first place?"

His father went quiet. He had dreams of his son being able to defend himself in front of twenty men. He thought his son could have a career in security, protecting the Emperor or assassinating the country's enemies. But he was losing his son's attention by the day, and his training was becoming weaker.

"Are you sure you want the life of an ordinary boy?"

"Yes. Yes I do."

"Then I will send word out. I will look for a replacement for you, a boy who is willing to be trained in the way of the ninja. It's all you've ever known, and so you don't realise its value. I will send you away, overseas, and you will taste what it is like to be born into another family, in a different culture, and you will return enriched from the experience."

"Another country? No, no I didn't mean…"

"Leave!" his father yelled. "I will find you a good home. I have connections with some people in England, a place that exists on the other side of the world. You will experience life there as a normal boy."

"Maybe I could still stay in Japan?"

"Leave!"

And the young ninja named Myasako left the dojo, looking down at the ground, wondering what he had just done.

Change

If we can yield to the changes of life,
we will become empowered by them.

Chapter 2 - Ninja Dreams

"Mum, mum I really want to be a ninja."

Martin, the other boy who lived in England, came into the kitchen dressed in his ninja uniform. He was throwing kicks and punches in the air and making noises with his voice.

"Ninjas are silent, dear."

"Well how do you know that? Have you ever met one?"

"Yes. I used to know one."

"What?" Martin ran up to his mum who was standing by the sink, and he grabbed her by the arm. "What do you mean you used to know one? Why didn't you ever tell me?"

"You never asked, dear," she said. "I spent time living with one once in Japan when I went travelling. He gave me a place to stay, and in return I helped him build his dojo."

"Wow, did you ever do any training?"

"No dear. I wasn't very interested, to be honest. When I saw him training, and training others, I never wanted to do it."

"Why not?"

"Because it's so hard, it's so intense. It is a complete way of life. They teach you to ignore pain."

"Cool."

"Do you know the only way to train yourself to ignore pain?"

"What?"

"You have to experience lots of it."

Martin kept jumping around the room, and a letter came in through the letterbox.

"I'll get it mum!" he yelled, and he stomped and jumped and kicked his way to the front door, and then rolled back and jumped up and gave the letter back to her. She began to open the letter and read it.

"Mum, I really don't want to just be like a normal kid anymore. I want to be different. I want to do ninja training in Japan like you could have done, I don't want to just run around and play games with Harry and all that lot, I want to learn how to fight, I want to learn how to use weapons and move silently and be just like those ninjas in the films."

"Darling," she said, putting down the letter. "Are you sure?"

*

She spent a while admiring the letter, the beautiful writing, the attention to detail, the absolute unhurriedness that was oozing out of it. The letter was like a piece of art. She wanted to frame it.

"Martin, I have a letter here from that very same man from Japan. I haven't heard from him in years. He knows that I have a young son, and he says *his* son has had enough with ninja training. He says he wants someone who he can trust to come to his home and train with him in exchange for his own son. For two weeks."

"Mum! Are you serious!?" Martin ran round and looked at the letter. It was so beautiful that he stared for a while. He wanted to meet whoever had written it. "Mum let me, let me, let me, let me!" Martin was jumping around her, up and down, until she tried to calm him down.

"You do realise, dear, that Japan is nothing like here. The food is different, the people are different, the culture...I mean, you're extremely loud dear, the Japanese aren't so...well...boisterous. You won't be allowed to jump around so freely in a dojo."

"Mum," Martin said, sounding very sure. "I've wanted to be a ninja all of my life."

His mother smirked.

"Let me go. It's only two weeks, just so I can try it."

"Alright dear, at least I'll know you'll be safe where you're going. I'll write back to him. I don't think he has a computer."

"Cool!" Martin yelled. "Thanks mum!" he said as he ran up the stairs, going to grab his foam-covered nunchuks.

*

Back in Japan, Myasako was practicing his kicks. He was kicking a punch bag in the same way for the hundredth time. Four hundred to go, then he could switch legs.

"Myasako!" his father called. "How many more?"

"Four hundred on this leg," he called back.

"Well, finish on that leg, and then on the other leg, and then come to see me."

Myasako kept kicking, painfully, for what felt like hours.

When he had finished his legs were wobbly, and he made his way out of the dojo to see his father in his office.

His father was sitting there, reading a letter.

"My son, you have been invited to go to England. An old friend who helped build this dojo is sending her son here, and she will take care of you for two weeks. You will need to go to school, but you will not need to do any training. You leave tomorrow. Go and pack your things."

Myasako bowed. The thought of no training made him feel light and relieved. Perhaps going to a different country would not be so bad if it meant a good rest.

With his aching, wobbly legs, he felt a deep sense of gratitude and excitement for the upcoming break from training that was now on the horizon, and he staggered slowly out of his father's office, with a very slight smile on his face.

Life

*When we accept the mysteriousness of life,
we align ourselves with its intelligence.*

Chapter 3 - Reality Check

Martin had begun packing.

"Right, I need shorts, t-shirts and trainers. I'll take my nunchuks, just in case he expects me to bring my own. What else do I need?"

"Toothbrush," his mum said.

"No, don't need that," Martin said. His mother put his toothbrush and some toothpaste in his suitcase.

"Towel, take a towel," she said. Martin grabbed a towel and threw it in his suitcase. His mother folded it up more neatly.

"Pants, socks," she said. He started throwing more clothes into the suitcase. His mother began to get covered in clothes.

"I'm not folding all of these up for you, Martin, fold them up yourself."

"They don't need folding, mum," he said. "Just push them in."

"Nope. I'm not doing it," she said, stepping back. Martin walked over and folded the pants and socks in a hurried, rushed way, so that none of them were folded properly. Then he closed up his suitcase, jumped on top of the bulging lid, and just managed to fasten it shut.

"There. All ready," he said.

*

Myasako did not have much to bring with him. He had two pairs of pants, two pairs of trousers, three shirts and a pair of nunchuks. Real ones, not foam ones. His father demanded that he take them.

He didn't tend to wear shoes, as his father thought it bred weakness, but his father gave him a pair, just in case.

"They might insist you wear these," he said. "If you live in someone's house you must respect their rules, and the lady you are living with might not have a cleaning bucket for your dirty feet when you enter the house. Take these."

The shoes were black and thin and light, and Myasako took them with reverence.

*

Neither of the boys had ever flown before. Each one of them stared out of the aeroplane windows, marveling at the clouds and the seas and the lands and the people below that were now so small that they became invisible to them. Neither could quite believe that they were hurtling through the air, when it felt as if they were sitting still.

When they arrived, both of them felt excited. Myasako felt excited for the rest and relaxation he was about to experience. Martin felt excited about all the ninja training he would get to do. They arrived on opposite sides of the globe, happy to escape their own lives for a while.

Martin was met outside the airport by a tall man dressed in black. He stood tall and firm and motionless. He bowed as Martin approached him.

"Martin?"

"Yes, hello."

"My name is Takashi. I will take you to where you are staying."

"Ok, thank you," Martin said, struggling with his luggage. "Do we have a taxi?"

"No, no taxi. We run. Your training begins now. You have lots and lots of baggage, so your journey will feel more heavy. First rule of the ninja – travel very lightly, not only on the outside, but on the inside too."

Martin didn't know what he meant. All he could feel was the weight of his suitcase that he was dragging behind him, and his backpack on his back full of sweets and fizzy drinks.

"Come!" Takashi called to Martin, already running off ahead. "Come, we run now!"

Martin could barely run whilst dragging his suitcase, but he tried. He ran through busy street markets where people were yelling and trying to sell him food. He saw Takashi in the distance gliding between people with ease, like his feet were making no impact with the ground. Martin was clunking and apologising and crashing into people, feeling exhausted already.

He was struggling to breathe freely, and after what seemed like hours of rummaging through the streets trying to keep site of Takashi, they eventually reached a clearing, out of the bustle of people, where there stood a small but grand little building, with stone pillars carved into the shape of dragons outside the hall.

"This is the dojo," Takashi said.

Martin had a headache. He was too hot, Japan was too hot, there were too many people, he had too much stuff, perhaps he should have never...

"Greetings," another man said, appearing at the entrance to the hall. He bowed. He was larger, thicker, more strongly built than Takashi, but he was dressed the same, in black, and he had a sword at his waist.

"My name is Kuyasaki. I am who you are to stay with. My son, Myasako, has travelled to stay with your mother. Welcome."

He bowed again.

"Thank you," Martin said, bowing but gasping for air at the same time.

"You need a drink," Kuyasaki said.

"Yes, thank you, I've got some here," Martin said, taking off his backpack, putting it on the dusty ground and opening it to reach for a can of soda. He pulled it out and cracked it open.

"Yame!" Kuyasaki cried. 'Yame' is Japanese for 'Stop', but Martin didn't know that. Still the deep noise of it felt like it went right into his body, and he stopped drinking.

Kuyasaki slipped some sandals on his feet to walk outside of the dojo. He trotted up to Martin and took the drink from him, then inspected his bag.

"What is this? Is this what you put inside your body?"

"Yeh," Martin said.

"Has your mother taught you nothing?"

"What do you mean?"

"Your body is made up of what goes in it. If you put rubbish in your body, your body will be rubbish. Come, we have fresh spring water inside, come."

Martin was dying for the sweetness of that drink that was now being carried away by the large ninja, and he was wishing that he was back at home with his mum.

Discipline

Wholesome self-discipline is a friend of the wise,
and an enemy of the weak.

Chapter 4 - A Strange New Place

When Myasako arrived in England, Martin's mother was waiting for him outside the airport.

"Hello, Myasako, my name is Amanda. Welcome to England."

Myasako bowed, as was his custom. Amanda bowed back. She never particularly liked shaking hands, but she usually felt as if it was rude not to.

They did not say much, Myasako just looked around. He looked at the sky and the people and the absence of people speaking Japanese. He felt a very long way from home.

Martin's mother made him Japanese food for dinner. It wasn't the same as when he was at home, but he appreciated it and said thank you many times. After they had eaten, Myasako could see some children out in the empty road, playing football.

He looked, and he yearned to play. Martin's mother saw him looking and yearning and said, "You can go out if you want to. But just for an hour. It's time to come in before it gets dark."

"Yes. Thank you, Amanda," Myasako said.

He walked outside, barefoot through habit, and he slowly walked up to the other children.

"Eh, there's the ninja kid!" one of them yelled. They all stopped playing football and ran up to Myasako. They surrounded him, and Myasako, without thinking, went into his ninja stance, low and ready.

"Woah!" the same kid said, "Woah, we're friends, not enemies."

Myasako was ready to strike.

"Stop surrounding him like this!" the same boy said. "Everyone just meet him from the front."

The boys and girls rearranged themselves, and they calmed down.

"I'm Harry, that's Glen, she's Ava and he's Michael. That's Helen over there."

There was one girl, Helen, sat far away from everyone else, sitting on the wall of a house garden, pointing her face at the floor. But Myasako could sense that she was looking up with her eyes at them.

All the children stood in front of Myasako, wide-eyed and smiling.

"So, you're a ninja," Harry said. "Can you show us some moves?"

Myasako was now standing normally.

"No. A ninja only uses his skills when he has to."

"Ok," Harry said. "What about football?"

"Never played."

Harry stumbled where he stood.

"You've never played football? Are you joking? Come on I'll show you."

At first, all Myasako could do was kick the ball as if it was a punch bag. It would fly off down the road and he would have to run to catch it and bring it back. Luckily he never got tired of running. His father would make him run every morning.

"No, kick it more gently, like this," Harry said, showing Myasako there was a different way to kick. Myasako didn't see the point of kicking something in this way, but he slowly got used to it, and began to enjoy the game.

*

Back in Japan, Martin was woken up at 4 a.m. by Kuyasaki, who was standing over him, poking him with a stick.

"Up. You run."

"What?"

"Run. Time to run. Ninja training starts at 4 a.m."

"Why this early?"

"Start when roads are empty and mind is empty. When roads are busy we do agility and awareness training. This is endurance training. Up, come."

Next to Martin's bed, Kuyasaki had laid out some light clothes and shoes for him to wear.

"I run with you today. Come."

"It's too early," Martin said, rolling over to go back to sleep.

Normally, Kuyasaki would have hit his son with a stick. He had promised Martin's mother, however, that he would never hit her son with a stick. Instead he used words.

"If you do not want to train as my son trains, as a ninja trains, then you must leave. There is no use you being here if you will not train correctly. Your mother said you wanted to be a ninja. Perhaps you want no such thing. Perhaps the ninja spirit is simply not within you."

Martin opened his eyes.

"Fine, Ok, I'm getting up," Martin said, eager to prove him wrong.

"Good, thank you," Kuyasaki said. "My boy normally runs seven miles. I do not expect you to train the same distance as him. But we must stick to his schedule."

"Ok then," Martin said, slipping on his lightweight clothes.

"Do you run at home?"

"I play football and catch."

"Ok, let's go."

Martin had not been up this early, ever. Not even at Christmas. There was something sacred about the early morning, something clear and quiet and holy. Still his body wanted to go back to sleep.

"Now we are running, we are only running. You need not think of anything else. We are running," Kuyasaki said. For such a large man, he didn't make any noise when he ran. He glided.

Martin started thinking about his flight home in two weeks.

"No need to think of that now," Kuyasaki said, as if he could read Martin's mind. "Just running. Empty streets, empty mind."

There was a thin mist around in the air still, and Martin's mind felt much mistier.

"What do you mean?" Martin said. "You mean think of nothing?"

"Not even that," Kuyasaki said.

"Well how do I not think of anything?"

"It is not how, but why," Kuyasaki said.

"Ok, why would I want to not think at all? Surely I need to?"

"Sometimes you do," Kuyasaki said. "But not always. Do you need to think about running, how to run, how to move your legs – or does it just happen? Usually all our thinking is a waste of energy. We do one thing, but then just worry about something else. Enjoy your running, that is all."

Ok, enjoy my running, Martin thought. He had a voice in his head that never stopped speaking. He could hear the voice, his thoughts, but he thought he *was* the voice. He thought every voice and image that arose in his head was who he was.

How can I enjoy it? He thought. I know, I'll think about home – that will make me happy. I wish I was back home right now, I miss my mum, I want to…

"Empty yourself of yourself," Kuyasaki said.

"What?"

Kuyasaki didn't respond.

"Just breathe," Kuyasaki said. "Breathing is very important. Fill yourself with breath."

Martin breathed in consciously, for two breaths, then he was thinking about what he would have for breakfast…

*

Soon Myasako was very good at football. He was faster, more agile and stronger than all of the other children, and he had great dexterity in his legs. Soon he was dribbling the ball around everyone and scoring goals.

"Woah, he's good," Harry said. "Maybe too good. Pass, remember to pass the ball!" Harry called to Myasako.

Myasako was confused. He was told that his team had to score goals. He was scoring goals much more efficiently than passing it around to other players who couldn't score goals. He didn't quite understand.

"We all want to play too you know!" Harry called after Myasako, who was about to shoot. Myasako passed him the ball, backwards, and still did not quite understand football.

"Reach your targets and goals as directly, easily and swiftly as possible," his father's voice was in his ears. "Do not listen to what anyone else says when they try to distract you or pull you down. If you see an honourable path to your goals, to the target, to strike, then take it. Forget everything else, as long as you remain honourable."

Myasako felt as if these children were not in any way interested in the ninja code.

*

After a mile and a half, Martin couldn't run anymore. Kuyasaki ended up carrying him home, and he threw him in a cold bath.

"Ahhh! It's cold!" Martin cried.

"Yes, helps your legs, strengthens your mind," Kuyasaki said. "Next part of ninja training. You'll get used to it."

Martin wanted to jump out. He tried, but Kuyasaki touched his shoulder and somehow his legs weakened, and he sat back in the water.

"I've still got clothes on!" Martin wanted a reason to get out of the cold.

"No matter, they will dry in the sun. You will not stay in for too long. Just thirty seconds, you can handle it."

Martin wanted a distraction.

"How long does your son stay in here for?"

"At least ten minutes. But be careful with comparisons. If you compare yourself to others, you will either feel inferior, or superficially superior. There is little wisdom in comparison."

Martin tried to talk about something else.

"Avoidance is a way of dealing with pain and discomfort," Kuyasaki said. "But until you accept them in their purity, they will always feel as if they dominate you."

"Is thirty seconds up yet?"

"Nearly. Yes, Ok, you can get out now."

Martin sprang up to his feet.

"Ah!" he said, feeling strangely invigorated. "So what next?"

*

"Did you enjoy football, dear?" Martin's mum said as Myasako walked in, exactly on the time she had requested. Normally she had to go out and call Martin, sometimes drag him back inside the house.

"Um, yes, I think so," Myasako said, unsure if he had really enjoyed it as much as the other children seemed to.

"Are you used to playing with other children?"

"No."

"Hmm," Martin's mother said. "Just bear in mind that your father has taught you to be a highly disciplined fighting machine, and children here are usually nothing like that. They are not super-serious about everything like your father is. They don't have so many goals."

Myasako sat, and listened.

"Do you have a dojo?" he asked.

She laughed and nearly spat out her tea by accident.

"No dear, we don't. We don't even have a punch bag. I did have a small one that Martin used to use, but he got bored with it after a while…"

"Everyone gets bored of the punch bag," Myasako said.

"Yes," she said, "but how few stick with it and reap the benefits?"

Myasako realised, for the first time, that what his father had taught him, might not be so bad after all...

That night it felt strange for Myasako to have done no martial arts training whatsoever. No meditation, no cold baths, no running through the streets. He thought he would feel free, more relaxed, but he actually felt almost itchy, like he was missing something. He couldn't rest properly. He had to get up in the middle of the night, stand in the middle of Martin's room and throw kicks and punches. He just had to do *some*, and then he felt better.

*

Martin was drinking water after the run.

"No more legs today," Kuyasaki said. "We must not over-train. When the body is tired, it is a good time for meditation. We will meditate in the dojo, and then do some fighting drills."

"Yeh, fighting drills!" Martin said, standing up and punching the air.

"First we meditate." Kuyasaki pointed Martin to sit back down.

"Ok," Martin said, closing his eyes. "How do we meditate? I've seen it in movies, but I don't know how."

"There is no how. Only why," Kuyasaki said.

Martin opened his eyes. "Why do you keep saying that?"

"Because if we know why, there is no how. How is made easy through why."

"So why do we meditate?"

"Rest, relaxation. Clarity. Peace. Insight. All things that are important to the true martial artist. But it is no use me just telling you. The 'why' must be realised."

"Why?"

Kuyasaki smiled. "We begin by not trying to tame our minds."

Martin closed his eyes. Doesn't make sense, he thought, I thought meditation meant no thoughts...

"If you try to stop a thought, it feels as if you are stuck to it, as if it is turning around to bite you. Thoughts are not to be clung to. They wish to pass through."

Martin was thinking about his friends. He didn't even *realise* he was thinking.

"At first we just sit here. We do nothing."

"How?" Martin interrupted.

"You are so trained in how. There is no how. Be aware of your breathing. Feel the stillness inside your body. Make that your focus, rather than thoughts being your focus. However, thoughts are not enemies."

"What's the aim here?" Martin interrupted again. "What should I be feeling?"

"The aim?" Kuyasaki said. "To, for a moment, be free from aims. That is meditation."

Martin sat, tensed up his body and mind, and tried to be free from aims.

Stillness

From stillness rises all things.

Chapter 5 - The Bully Named Arthur Muldridge

The next morning, Myasako was woken up by Martin's mother.

"Myasako! Time for breakfast, and then it's time for school."

Myasako was not used to going to school. He was normally home-schooled by his father. The idea of going to school with other children was very strange to him.

"The bus will come to pick you up in one hour," she said as they sat and ate breakfast together.

"Do you not run in the mornings?" Myasako asked.

Martin's mother shook her head as she drank some orange juice.

"No dear, never."

Myasako felt uncomfortable. He thought he would feel so relieved to not need to run in the mornings, but without his normal regime, he felt slightly uneasy.

"What about meditation?" he said, looking at all the food she had prepared. He was not hungry.

"I meditate sometimes," she said, "but I've gotten out of the habit recently."

"Ok," he said, eating something out of politeness, but wishing, strangely, that he was just back home in his normal routine.

"Cheer up, Myasako! Are you missing home?"

"Not home," Myasako said. "But my way of life."

"Well, you've always got time for a quick meditate before school if you like. Actually, no you don't, we still have to pack your bag and your clothes for PE and your lunch. Meditation will have to wait."

And then Myasako's father's voice rang in his ears. It said:

"Myasako, meditation is for here and now, any time and any place."

And so Myasako looked around, breathed consciously, and felt a little less lost.

*

"One thousand punches," Kuyasaki said.

"What?" Martin said. He was used to throwing three or four and then doing something else.

"One thousand punches." Kuyasaki said. "Not full power. Just work on technique. Like this..."

Kuyasaki walked up to a punch bag in the dojo, stood in his ninja stance, and threw a lightning fast jab of a punch at the bag, which left a dent in the side. Martin nearly didn't see it.

"That was fast!" Martin said, excited. "How do you get to be that fast?"

"Repetition. Skill is built by repetition," Kuyasaki said. "One thousand of those. Five hundred on each arm. If you throw them with full power, you will get tired too easily. No need to be so powerful yet. Just throw them like this..."

Kuyasaki demonstrated much more slowly how the punch would explode out from his body like a snake, and then recoil back after impact.

"Throw the punch, through the bag as if the bag is not there," he said, demonstrating again. "You try now."

Martin got in his own ninja stance. He threw a punch. It was rubbish, he thought. It felt weak and slow and soft compared to Kuyasaki's.

"Be careful of your comparisons with others!" Kuyasaki warned. "They can deceive and discourage. Just be yourself."

"But I'm so slow compared to you!" Martin insisted.

"Everyone must be a beginner at some point," Kuyasaki said. "The difference between a master and a student, is that the master has practiced more times than the student. That is the only difference. He has pushed through difficulty, the beginner stage, the intermediate stage and beyond. He continues to dedicate himself to his craft, and as a result his craft rewards him with greater skills. But you must accept where you are, without getting stuck there. If you resist where you are, you will be stuck."

Martin stared at the bag. He still had nine hundred and ninety-nine punches to throw.

"You can only throw one punch at a time. You are obsessed with speed and flashiness so that you can feel better about yourself. But correct technique is learnt through slowness. A great master once said that slow is smooth, and smooth is fast. We must begin slow. We must learn to love the punch, love the movement, become friends with it, and it will begin to yield to us its secrets."

Martin settled slightly and threw a little more slowly.

"Slower!" Kuyasaki demanded. All Martin wanted to do was get through this exercise so he could rest and do something else.

"The more you strive away from yourself and what you are doing, the more you will suffer. Surrender to the process."

Martin felt annoyed. He expected to be doing kicks and flips and weapons training by now, climbing up walls and jumping off roofs and landing with ease. This isn't what he thought it would be.

"Your expectations! Leave them at the door!" Kuyasaki barked. Martin just kept punching, more slowly than he had ever punched before.

*

Myasako was waiting for the school bus. It felt good to be outside. When it arrived for him he could sense Martin's mother moving away from the window of the house, and moving her attention back inside. He was aware of so many things that other people weren't aware of. He could feel someone looking at him from many houses away, he could hear things that were too far away to see, and he could see things in such detail, that everything seemed to have a personality of its own.

The bus that arrived seemed tired, old and grumpy. It didn't like being painted yellow. The bus was loud and arrived on the road by his feet. The door opened and the smelly driver was sitting there, chewing gum and staring at Myasako blankly. He didn't smile at all.

Myasako climbed aboard and looked at the children. Everyone looked at him.

He walked past children who were whispering and pointing, and eventually he found a seat by himself. But he didn't feel as if it was a safe one.

Behind him was one of the school bullies. His name was Arthur Muldridge, a boy with a rich dad who gave him anything and everything he demanded. He was bigger than the other children, and fatter, because he could not stop eating puddings and sweets. Myasako could feel Arthur looking at him from behind, and he felt he had to adjust himself so he didn't have his back to Arthur. He put his back to the window of the bus, away from the chair.

"You're Martin's replacement aren't ya?" Arthur said, appearing over and behind the chair of Myasako. "You look weird, not like the rest of us. Why do you look so strange?"

Myasako didn't have an answer.

"I asked you a question!" Arthur yelled at Myasako, and before Arthur even knew what he was going to do, Myasako could feel a warning that his shirt was about to be grabbed. Myasako moved himself, and as Arthur went to grab him, Myasako wasn't there. Arthur became confused.

"Come here and answer me!" Arthur said again. This time Myasako didn't have any more room to adjust, and as Arthur's big greedy hands reached in to grab his shirt, Myasako took Arthur's hands and twisted them into a wrist lock.

"Ow! Ow let go!" Arthur yelled. The whole school bus was watching and starting to laugh. Arthur was twisted around so that he was lying on top of the back of the seat, his arm and wrist twisted behind him by Myasako.

"Get off!" Arthur yelled again.

"You must leave me alone," Myasako said, calmly. "Do you agree?"

"Yeh, yeh sure," Arthur said.

Myasako released him, Arthur cowered back into his own seat, and for the rest of the journey Myasako sat on the bus, alone.

When he arrived at school Myasako was greeted by a girl his age.

"Hi Myasako!" she said. She was blonde and pretty. Myasako had never interacted much with girls before.

"Myasako my name is Laura. I'm one of Martin's friends and I normally meet him here when he gets off the bus. Are you enjoying your time in England?"

"I'm not sure," Myasako said. "Not as much as I thought I would."

"Well, hopefully you'll enjoy today," she said. "Come on, come and meet some of my other friends."

Laura took Myasako by the hand, and led him off to meet some other children.

*

"I've still got eight hundred to go. This is so boring!" Martin said. "Can't I just throw these punches quickly and get it over with?"

Kuyasaki sat down cross-legged, next to Martin on the floor of the dojo.

"Why are you here?" he said to Martin.

"To learn to be a ninja."

"Why do you want to be a ninja?"

"So I can do cool stuff and fight people off who bully me like Arthur Muldridge at school."

"You get bullied?"

"Sometimes. I don't know what to do if someone grabs me or tries to punch me."

"What's more important to you..." Kuyasaki said. "Learning how to fight someone off, or doing cool stuff?"

Initially Martin thought of doing cool stuff, of being praised by his friends, of Laura thinking he was so cool. All of that felt very nice. Then he thought of being able to defend himself. That felt even better.

"How to fight someone off if I have to," Martin said.

"Ok!" Kuyasaki said. "We have found your 'why'. Now we know the main reason you are here. Before you thought you wanted to be a real ninja. Really you just want some fighting tools. Are there not any places near your home where they teach you things like that?"

"Maybe. My mother has suggested it. But I always thought I had to go to a proper ninja place..."

"Hmmm..." Kuyasaki said. "Ok. Then we will tailor our training to what you want most. The true ninja way can be learnt later. But for now, this is what you do if someone grabs you by the shirt..."

*

At lunch time, Myasako was playing football again. He still didn't quite understand it, but he found that he enjoyed it more when he didn't take it so seriously. Suddenly his ninja senses started to tingle, and he could feel a threat coming from behind him. He ducked and covered his head and he felt the weight of Arthur Muldridge come flying over him. Arthur had tried to catch him by surprise, but Myasako moved around Arthur, and crouched down low.

"The element of surprise is crucial to the ninja way," his father said in his mind. "The best attack comes from nothing."

Myasako relaxed his stance. He looked more normal, standing there with one arm folded across his body, and one arm folded on top, with his hand looking like it was picking his own nose.

"Come here!" Arthur yelled, and he trundled towards Myasako, who darted off to the side and kicked at Arthur's knee as he ran forwards, leaving Arthur to crash into the floor very hard, and cut his face.

"An enemy must be reasoned with until he can no longer be reasoned with," Myasako's father said in his head.

"Can we not just be friends?" Myasako said.

"No way," Arthur said. He now had a bad leg and a cut face but he ran towards Myasako, and just as a teacher appeared in the distance, to the right of them, with kids beginning to crowd around and shout, Myasako kicked Arthur straight in the gut, and when he did he felt something burst inside of Arthur's stomach, and Arthur keeled over, and started to cry.

"Myasako!" A teacher came running out and grabbed Myasako by the wrist. Without thinking, he reversed her grip and flipped her over so that she landed softly on her back and let him go. And then as more teachers started to run out of the school to stop whatever fight was going on, Myasako ran, faster than any child had ever been seen to run, and he disappeared into the woods behind the school.

*

"Ok, thanks, I've learnt that now, what next, what about if I get grabbed from behind?" Martin said to his new teacher, Kuyasaki, back in Japan.

"Hang on, not so fast," Kuyasaki said. "You've only done it twice. The key to this is repetition. You cannot escape it. We have to do it many times so that your muscles remember it, not just your thinking mind. It needs to be automatic, a reflex that gets built into your system so that you don't have to think. In a real fight, there is not enough time for thinking, the reflex has to be there."

"Ok, fine!" Martin said. He didn't realise how impatient he was.

"You must realise that for any skill to be obtained in this life means that you must fall in love with the process of practicing it. If you want a magic spell to be done where you suddenly have all the powers and skills of a ninja, then you will always be frustrated while you are here. This takes work and commitment and dedication. There is no way around it."

"Do you know any spells?" Martin said.

"Maybe," Kuyasaki said. "But they are only for the experienced ninjas."

*

Later that day, Martin's mother received a phone call. It was the voice of a disgruntled teacher.

"Hello, Mrs Davies, I'm afraid your exchange student, Myasako, has gone missing. He was caught fighting in the playground and ran off. We can't find him anywhere. Would you mind coming in?"

"Ok," Martin's mother said. "But you do realise he's a ninja? If he doesn't want to be found, he won't be found. Who was he fighting with?"

"Arthur Muldridge."

"The one that bullies my son who always seems to get away with it? The one with the father who gives the school money?"

There was no response.

"I will come in," she said, "but I'm very well glad that he gave that bully a good beating. He deserves it."

She slammed down the phone and went to fetch her coat, and Myasako was sitting on the stairs. She nearly jumped out of her skin.

"Oh! Myasako! How did you get in the house?"

"Have I done a bad thing?" Myasako said, ignoring her question. "The teachers began to chase me."

"Not at all," Martin's mother said, going over and putting her arm around the boy. "Not at all."

強さ

Strength

*To attain physical strength,
mental strength is required.*

Chapter 6 - Martin's Danger

Myasako was not allowed back at the school for the rest of his time in England. He was, however, invited over to Arthur Muldridge's house by his father, Jacobson Muldridge.

Jacobson appeared at the door of Martin's mother's house, two days after the fight at school. He was tall, dressed in a dark purple suit with slicked-back hair and a smile that made him look evil.

"Myasako?" he said, holding his hand out to shake it. Myasako ignored the hand, but bowed. He didn't know what handshaking even meant.

"Myasako I would like you to come to my house for a meal. I feel as if you and Arthur have gotten off on the wrong foot, and I would like you two to become friends. Would that be possible? I have a chef who is Japanese, who cooks the finest Japanese cuisine. Would you like to come?"

"No," Myasako said.

"I was hoping you could share your philosophies with me and Arthur. Arthur tells me you attacked him. Other children say he attacked you. I would like to invite you over for dinner, so this can be settled and we can share a little of our cultures. Tomorrow night. You can bring Martin's mother too, if you like."

"Would this mean that Arthur no longer picks on Martin at school?" Martin's mother said, standing next to Myasako.

"Of course. Arthur will never lay a finger on poor Martin again," Jacobson smiled.

"Ok, we will come then," she replied.

"Excellent." Jacobson smiled again, bowed slightly and turned back to go and sit in his Rolls Royce, which had the driver standing outside of it, ready to open the door.

Myasako still didn't want to go. He had a terrible feeling in his bones about this man. It was the way he smiled, or the way his hair was too slicked back, or the way he walked or the way he spoke. Something unsettled him. Something seemed dishonest, and his ninja senses told him that he must go into Jacobson and Arthur's house that night, to see what they really had planned.

*

"Where are all the other kids?" Martin said. "I miss having friends to play with. Where is the school?"

"The nearest school is far away from here," Kuyasaki replied. "There are not many children your age, either. You may see some occasionally, but rarely on this street."

Martin looked out onto the empty dirt road outside, with the bustle of the market beyond it.

"You are to be home-schooled while you are here," Kuyasaki said. "I feel that martial arts should be a significant portion of a child's education. We also devote three hours a day to Maths, English and Martial History."

"What about Science?"

"We do Science on a Friday and Wednesday."

Martin felt trapped. He wanted to go to more places, see more things. His legs already felt numb from this morning's run, and although he had learnt what to do when people would attack him, he still felt as if something was missing – the company of others his age.

"I can't believe you keep your son here like this. Surely he needs to have more friends."

"The ninja's life must be a solitary one."

"Why?"

"It builds character."

"But so do friends!" Martin said. "Don't you ever feel like he is missing out on things?"

"Yes. Of course," Kuyasaki said. "But what he loses in fun, he gains in mastery."

"And you think mastery is more important than fun?" Martin said. He was feeling agitated and even more trapped, like he just had to leave. "Where are my shoes!" he cried. "I have to leave."

"Do not leave by yourself, you do not know these streets," Kuyasaki warned.

"I'm leaving, I'm going to find some fun. I thought ninja life would be fun. But it's not. It's boring and hard and repetitive."

"You want the fruits, but you do not want to care for the tree," Kuyasaki said.

"What are you talking about!" Martin cried. "What fruits? What tree? Just let me go!"

Martin pushed past his master, and he walked out into the street. He turned right, and disappeared from view, but he could be heard stomping down the street for many minutes by Kuyasaki, who was pausing to wonder if he was truly doing what was best for his own son.

*

That night Myasako dressed himself in black. He had a pair of slip-on shoes that his father had given to him, and he took out his nunchuks from his suitcase.

"Weapons are not to be clung to, and only used when necessary," his father said in his head. "Do not use your skills when they are not needed."

Myasako looked out into the night. It was two o'clock in the morning, and he put his nunchuks inside a small cloth bag with a string that he tied around his shoulder and body, and he stood again, staring into the night.

"I have to go to Muldridge's house," he thought. "I have to see what he really has planned for us. This is the time to use my skills for good." He approached the window, gently opened it, leapt from his bedroom onto a nearby tree, and clambered down the tree like a little ape, and he disappeared silently down the road, and into the night.

He had found out where Muldridge's house was from asking Martin's mother...

"You know the grassy park that the bus drove past on your way to school? By the side of the park there's a road that leads up the big hill near the swings. We keep going up the hill and then the house is at the very top, just on the right. It has a big driveway and a big gate at the front, it's called 'Muldridge Hills'."

Myasako never mentioned he was going to go there alone in secret, and after running through the dark empty streets, he was soon running alongside the park. Once he had cleared the park he saw the narrow road near the swings which led up the hill and away from town. He started running up it.

The night air was cold and biting, but Myasako had always been taught to breathe through it. He could even direct heat to certain areas of his body, just by thinking about it. He was running up the hill as if he had only just begun running, not letting up any pace, and soon he arrived at a gated estate, huge tall gates with spikes on the top, with a long and winding driveway surrounded by trees which led to a large mansion in the distance.

Myasako looked up at the gate. He could even see a security guard's office just inside to the left, and then he noticed two surveillance cameras staring down at him, blankly.

Myasako darted off to the side and rolled into the trees by the side of the lane, and he started to move through the trees, around the gate that had turned into a huge iron fence surrounding the land of Jacobson Muldridge, and Myasako started to look for an opening.

*

Martin was walking along, feeling sorry for himself.

"I want to go home," he said out loud. "I don't even want to be around Kuyasaki. All he'll do is make me do drills and make me work and make me run. I don't want to be a ninja at all. What's the point?"

The road he was walking along was empty and quiet. He was alone. He had left the bustle of the marketplace and the little town, and he was suddenly aware that everything around him was very quiet.

His mind had been a storm of suffering, of feeling sorry for himself, of wishing he was somewhere else, until suddenly he noticed that it was all very quiet indeed.

He was alone. There was silence everywhere. Nothing was really happening. His torturous mind left him like a cloud being blown away, and suddenly he was like the pure sky, empty and clear, and even slightly happy.

It wasn't his normal happiness. It was cooler than that. He felt spacious, as if all of his thoughts had been like dreams, and he looked around at the empty road, not needing to think about anything at all.

And then, in the distance, he heard the engine of a van.

Something in him tingled and told him to move away, to hide, but he ignored it slightly. He looked for places to hide and then thought:

"Don't be silly, no need to hide, I'm only on a road. No, I think I'll go back to Kuyasaki and apologise for storming out like that. Suddenly, without all of my old thoughts, I feel much better about all of this."

The tingling in him got stronger. He started to walk back to where he had come from, and he could see the van in the distance getting closer.

"Hide!" he heard Kuyasaki say from the middle of his chest. "Hide!"

The tingling in his body and fingers became so strong that he found himself running off the road, along a dry and barren field that led back to the town.

"Run faster!" the voice inside of him said.

Martin ran faster and faster, but he wasn't used to running at such speeds for so long, and although he had adrenaline beginning to pump through his veins, giving him bursts of energy, he could feel himself slowing down.

"Look behind you," the voice inside him said, and he turned whilst running to see the van steer off the road, on to the field, and begin chasing him down.

"It's too late," Martin thought. "I'm too far away to hide anywhere. I have to fight. Oh, I wish I was better at fighting, I should have just stayed and trained with Kuyasaki."

Martin stopped and looked at the van, but then decided that all he could do was run anyway, until the van was soon on him, rumbling the ground and his eardrums, driving in front of him and screeching to a halt, and four men in masks jumped out, grabbed him, and threw him in the back of the van. The four men jumped in after him and the van sped off again, turning around, and driving back on to the road.

*

They were all speaking Japanese, the men. Martin couldn't understand any of it. It sounded aggressive and harsh and panicked. He heard the occasional word "Kuyasaki", but couldn't understand anything else. His hands were tied behind his back, and he was lying on the floor of the van. He was scared.

"Where are you taking me?" Martin asked one of them.

They ignored him. They carried on talking amongst themselves, and Martin had a terrible dark feeling begin to sink down inside his chest as he realised that these men didn't care about his welfare at all.

"Where are we going?" Martin said again. This time one of the men looked at him. They all still had their masks on, and Martin could see that in the corner of this man's eye, there was a thick scar that led into the side of his mask.

The man started to laugh. All the other men stopped talking and started to laugh, too. But then they stopped. They started looking at Martin more closely in the darkness of the back of the van, and the man with the scar beside his eye stood up from his seat and approached Martin on the floor. The man knelt down and moved his face towards Martin's.

"Myasako?" The man grunted, staring with a wild gaze straight into Martin's now clearly English, un-Japanese looking face.

"No!" Martin shook his head. "No I'm not Myasako!"

The man stood up. He shouted at the rest of the men, and mentioned the name "Myasako!" again. The man was pointing at Martin's face, and all the men looked and leaned in closer to look at Martin, all realising that they had kidnapped the wrong boy.

"You were in dojo! You left dojo and we followed you!" the scarred man said. "You were with Kuyasaki!"

"But I'm not Myasako!" Martin cried. He could feel his insides shaking, he felt so afraid and exposed with his hands tied behind his back. He thought of his mum.

The man screamed and started punching the walls of the old van, which was steering and screeching its way through the roads at a consistent pace.

Then the man stopped, and he stared at the floor. Then he sat down, and he looked at Martin again.

"We still take you. Kuyasaki might still pay *lots* to get you back."

The man's eyes became smaller in his mask as he smiled an evil smile, and a wave of sniggering flowed through the rest of the men.

"Yes," the man said. "We still take you."

And with a fearful pit of darkness inside Martin's chest, they drove him further and further away from the dojo, to a place he did not know.

恐
怖

Fear

*Fear is an energy we must
accept in order to overcome.*

Chapter 7 - Infiltration

Whilst Myasako was running around, through the forest, scanning the perimeter of the Muldridge residence, he noticed a flaw in the property's defences. High up above him, at the top of the fence, one of the defensive spikes was broken. He looked up and pondered, and wondered what he might do next.

I need rope, he thought, looking around the forest floor.

As he looked around, he heard something. A car. The engine was getting louder as it was being driven up the lane towards the house. Myasako ran towards the sound, as quickly and as silently as he could, dodging trees and jumping over fallen branches and logs, and he saw the Rolls Royce of Jacobson Muldridge approaching the main gate.

Myasako got closer and approached as closely as he could without being seen, as he saw the main gates slowly begin to open. Myasako crouched down on to all fours, like an ape, and in the darkness he managed to sneak in behind the car, and as the car drove forward, in through the gates and past the security office, Myasako ran in behind it and darted off to the side behind the small building. Inside sat a security guard, going back to lazily read his newspaper after standing to attention, alert and saluting at the shiny car that was being driven in through the gates.

Myasako thought for a moment of dealing with the security officer, but he did not want to hurt anyone unnecessarily. He made sure he was absolutely silent, and moved away from the small building, and began running across the floodlit grass towards the house.

His heart was racing as he knew he might be seen, but he had to count on no one looking at the surveillance cameras at that moment. He reached some bushes closer to the house, and he could see through the gaps, Jacobson Muldridge was getting out of the car. It was 3 a.m., and Jacobson was known in town for being nocturnal, doing all of his business during the night, and as the driver and his staff at the door of the house were looking away, paying attention to Jacobson, Myasako darted through the bushes, up to the house, and managed to squeeze in through a small open window.

He was in a grand room. There was a large shiny piano in there, and in the middle, an even larger dining table.

Myasako stepped behind the huge curtains that were drawn to the side of the window he was standing at, and he collected his feelings.

He wasn't out of breath, but he was intensely alert, he could sense people moving through the house – three people's footsteps, and soon he could hear Jacobson speaking.

"Go and wake up Pablo, would you?" he said. "I fancy listening to some music while I eat. When will the food be ready?"

"Just five minutes sir, just five minutes," said a grovelling voice of a low-stooped and withered butler named Ellison.

"Well hurry up, I'm hungry," Jacobson said. "Where is my boy?"

"Asleep, sir, he is still very tired after his operation."

Jacobson entered the grand room that Myasako was standing in the corner of.

"I can't wait until I get my hands on that little Japanese boy that did that to him," Jacobson said. "Can you imagine that? Kicking my son so hard that he required surgery to fix his stomach? He could have died."

He sat down at the head of the large dining table. A maid put a napkin in his lap. Jacobson continued speaking.

"They confirmed that they would be coming tomorrow. The mother seemed more keen than the child, but I'm sure they will come. I gave them the promise that Arthur wouldn't touch that wimp of a boy Martin, and that's what sealed it for her. You should have seen her face light up at the prospect of Arthur no longer giving the boy any hassle! I can't wait to bring them both here. They will pay for what they've done to my boy."

At that moment, Arthur appeared at the door. He was being wheeled on a bed by an exhausted-looking maid, and he was eating a giant chocolate bar.

"Dad? Dad I stayed up to wait for you. I demanded I come downstairs to see you. Maid! Get me a drink!"

"You should be sleeping," Jacobson said, sitting down at the table.

"What did they say? Are they coming?" Arthur said, taking another huge bite from his chocolate bar.

"Yes my boy, yes they are."

Ninja

The ninja flows with whatever happens,
and so is carried by the moment.

Chapter 8 - Ninjas At Work

When the van carrying Martin finally came to a halt, the men inside all waited. It was dark where they were, inside the back of the van there were no windows, only angry Japanese voices which continued to argue about what they were to do with Martin. Two said wait for a ransom. One said put him to work in their factory. Another said it was too risky to keep him, that they would be caught soon enough.

Martin heard the driver get out of the door at the front of the van and shut it behind him. Another passenger, sitting next to the driver up front, did the same.

They walked around to the back of the van, and Martin noticed that they were taking their time.

As the doors opened behind them, Martin and the others were temporarily blinded by the brightness of the light, not only from the sun but from a lamp that was being shone on top of all of them. All of the men recoiled and yelled and complained that it was far too bright for them to see after sitting in the dark, but before they could finish complaining, they were being hit with sticks. They were being hit so hard and so quickly that they were being knocked unconscious, going limp and falling on the floor of the van, falling on top of Martin so that he was being squashed and was having trouble breathing. All Martin could hear was whacks of sticks and shouts of the men being attacked in the van, and soon his world had gone from bright to dark, and the final man's body fell on top of his head.

"Get them off him!" he heard a familiar voice say. "Drag them off before they squash him!"

As the men's bodies were dragged away, and the lamp was turned off behind them, Martin's eyes adjusted to see Kuyasaki, and the thin man from the airport, Takashi, dragging men out of the van, with wooden sticks tied to their waists.

"Hello, Martin," Kuyasaki said.

"It was you? You were driving the van? You came and captured me?"

"No," Kuyasaki said, heaving another man out of the van and dumping him on the ground. "No. We saw you had been captured. We followed you after you left to keep an eye on you. Then we ambushed the van and overpowered the driver."

"How? When?"

"Five minutes after you were captured."

"But I didn't hear you. How did you do that?"

"You wouldn't have heard us, that is the whole point of being a ninja. People don't know you have attacked them until it is too late, and I know these roads better than any van driver. It was an ambush, but I cannot reveal my secrets to you. Not yet, anyway. I heard them talking in the van, I knew they would not hurt you until they had been advised by their superiors."

Kuyasaki grabbed another limp body and began dragging it out of the van.

"Who do they work for?" Martin said, rubbing his eyes and standing up.

"My brother, Senzi. He left the way of the ninja a long time ago, and he has been trying to harm me in some way ever since."

"Why did you let me go?"

"You wanted to go."

"But you could have stopped me."

"Perhaps, but sometimes children have to learn lessons directly, rather than simply being warned of dangers that they do not even believe to be real. If I had told you that my brother's men might try to capture you, thinking you were my son, you would not have believed me. You would have probably ran out during the night to get away, and I would not have been able to save you."

"Have they ever tried to capture your boy?"

"No. But I see their scouts. I knew they were planning something. That is one reason why I train my son so hard, so that he can protect himself when the time comes."

"Ok," Martin said. "I'm sorry I left, forget what I said. Let's train again. I'll do whatever you want. Let's train, I don't care how repetitive it is. Let's train."

"Good," Kuyasaki said, dusting off his hands as Takashi dragged the bodies away. "Good. Let's do it."

*

"Hello Myasako, you're up early," Martin's mother said, the next morning. She came downstairs to see Myasako sitting there at the table, doing nothing.

"I have something to warn you about," Myasako said.

"What, dear?"

"I went to Muldridge's house last night. They are planning something bad for us."

"What did you say, dear?"

"I went to their house. They are planning bad things, they want revenge for what I did to that bully Arthur."

"Oh goodness, Myasako," Martin's mother said, walking in to the kitchen. "I know you don't want to go tonight, but surely your father has told you enough about telling fibs?"

"Fibs?"

"Yes, dear. You know, lies, lies to keep yourself from doing something you don't want to do. Martin does it sometimes."

Myasako rose from his chair.

"Mrs Davies, I'm sorry, but you misunderstand me. I actually did go. I broke into their home and heard them speaking."

She stopped at the fridge and looked at him.

"When?"

"Three in the morning."

"How? How did you get there?"

"I ran."

"And you heard what?"

Myasako explained again what he saw and heard.

She looked down at the floor.

"Oh, you sound just like Martin," she said. "He has all these games and fantasies too. Ok then, Myasako, so what will we do when we get there? What will we do, fight to the death? Ambush them?"

"This is not a game," Myasako said. "We must not go."

"Oh come on, dear. He's not going to do anything. I know you are a young ninja but I highly doubt you can break into a gated estate with security cameras and just wait in the corner while the richest man in town has a conversation with his boy about the terrible things he has planned for us. Your father maybe, but you are only young."

"Madam, do not go."

"I'm going," she said. "It's the only way I can get Arthur to stop bullying Martin."

Safety

Be grateful if you have a safe place to live, and a safe family to be a part of.

Chapter 9 - True Learning

"I'm getting it now," Martin said, as they were working on a flinch reflex to defend against punches.

"Yes, you are. Now we'll practice faster, move around. I will throw punches from different angles. You must defend."

The two were moving around the dojo, Kuyasaki started to throw open handed strikes quickly but lightly at Martin's forehead, and Martin was jamming the strikes with his own arms.

"Good, good," Kuyasaki said. "Faster."

Kuyasaki threw punches faster, and faster, and faster, until Martin could defend himself without thinking, he could stop a punch without needing to think about what to do, and after a while he was becoming out of breath.

"Ten more seconds, fight when you're tired!" Kuyasaki said, throwing blistering strikes at Martin's head, and Martin was moving his head, putting his hands up and defending, and he was picking it all up very quickly.

"Good, stop," Kuyasaki said, and Martin stepped back and relaxed his arms.

"Very good. See, soon it becomes natural, and then it becomes enjoyable."

"Yes, I see now," Martin said. "Thank you."

The two bowed at each other and walked over to a corner of the dojo where the floor was not matted, but stone. They sat down to drink water from cups.

"What happened with your brother? Why does he want to harm you?" Martin said.

Kuyasaki paused, and sipped his water.

"We had an arrangement where we both had some money invested in a particular project. When he left us and the dojo, he sold his shares in the project to me so that he could have some fast cash. Since then the value of my shares rocketed, making me wealthy in finances, and he has always regretted it. Regret will drive a man to madness, if he does not know how to deal with it."

"How do you deal with it, how do you deal with regrets?"

"You first accept the energy of regrets. You accept that you feel regret, rather than trying to fight against it. The fighting, the running from yourself and your feelings is what drives a person mad. So the first thing is to be comfortable with the feeling, to not turn it into an enemy."

"Then what?"

Kuyasaki paused again.

"Then you will see that the regret is almost an addictive thing. It feels bad, but it feels good. It's like someone who loves to talk and think about their problems. They don't like it, but secretly they do."

Martin paused this time.

"So then what? Is that it?"

"Then you will see that the regret is not a useful thing. It eats and festers in the body and mind, but it does not change the past or the future for the better. It just creates unhappiness."

"What about learning from your mistakes?"

"This is easy to do. Very easy. The regret and the guilt or the shame or the self-torture are completely extra. Optional extras. If you decide to simply regret nothing, because you no longer have the time to suffer in this life, then this will also help a great deal."

"Regret nothing?"

"Yes. Try it. You may have been trained in the power of regret, but all regret does is keep you stuck in the past, doomed to repeat what you never wanted. How we feel now affects our future. If you regret nothing, your life has a power and a freshness and a space for evolution. If you like to regret things, then it will feel as if you have chains tying you back to inevitable actions that you don't desire. This world is mental."

"Mental? You mean like crazy?"

"No. Thought-based."

At that moment an echoing gong rang from another room. It was time to eat, and the two stood up, bowed, walked to the exit of the dojo, and bowed again before they left.

武
道

Martial Arts

The true martial artist is peaceful,
yet capable of anything.

Chapter 10 - Myasako's Bravery

That night Martin's mother, Amanda, went alone to Jacobson Muldridge's house.

"Will you not come?" she asked Myasako as he sat on the stairs.

"No. Do not go," he said to her again. He wondered whether he should incapacitate her for her own good.

"People must make their own choices in life," his father rang in his heart.

"Ok, well they'll be very disappointed, and so am I," Martin's mother said. She stopped as she opened the door to leave.

"Don't you want to protect me?" she asked, turning around and smiling.

"Yes. So I will not accompany you," Myasako said, sitting a little bit taller on the stairs.

"See you later tonight, unless you're asleep," she said. "Then I'll see you tomorrow, Myasako."

"Goodnight," Myasako said, and she closed the door behind her.

As soon as she left, Myasako ran upstairs, got his bag with his nunchuks and an old rope he had found in the woods, and he leapt out of the window again, climbed down the tree, and as Martin's mother was getting into her car below him, she shut the door and he silently climbed on top. He had been taught to tread as if his feet and hands were kissing the surface that he was crawling on, and as he got on top of the car, he didn't make a sound, and was not seen in the darkness of the evening by Martin's mother.

The car drove and he clung his vice-like fingers onto the edges of the car where the doorframes were.

"A ninja's grip is paramount!" his father had said to him. Myasako had an image of all those hours of training his finger strength, hanging from rings and bars by just the tips of his fingers, doing push-ups on his fingers, striking walls with his fingers, climbing up ropes and hanging there by one arm.

"The grip is essential, not only with the fingers but with the toes!" his father always used to tell him.

With bare feet, Myasako was clinging onto the rear doorframes as well, wrapping his feet and toes into any grooves in the doorframes he could find, and he was sprawled out on top of the car, like a spider locked into position, and he was driven away from the house through the roads, past the park, and up the lane towards the Muldridge residence.

As the car approached the gate Myasako rolled off and followed in low as the car slowed down. The security guard came out of the office and shone a light on to Martin's mother, and asked her who she was. She explained herself, politely. The gate opened and as she drove through the gate, Myasako did the same thing as before. He ran in using the car as cover, and he rolled away from view of the security guard behind the building. He was by the door of the security guard's office, and the guard walked around to get back in through the door. Suddenly he was tripping over the outstretched leg of Myasako, and Myasako gripped the man at a certain point on the neck and pinned him down to the ground. The man soon passed out, but was still alive, and Myasako dragged the man back into the office, took away his walkie-talkie, his mobile phone, and using the rope in his bag, he tied the security officer to the corner of the room, on the floor.

"I'm sorry," Myasako said to him as he left, bowing to the man, and he took the man's keys from his belt line, moved his phone and walkie-talkie well away from him, and locked the guard in the office from the outside. He looked around, pocketed the keys, then sprinted again across the grass, and was soon in the bushes near the house.

He watched as Martin's mother got out of her car.

"Amandaaah..." Jacobson was at the door, and he greeted her with a sly smile as she approached him.

"Hello," she said, smiling slightly, and soon he had embraced her with one cold arm, and they were walking together into the house.

Myasako glided towards the same window as before. It wasn't open but it was unlocked again, and he popped it open, slid inside the house and closed it behind him.

The two parents were walking through the house together.

Just as Myasako went to hide behind the curtain, he noticed in the corner of the room was Arthur Muldridge, lying on a bed, staring up at the ceiling.

Myasako froze. When he saw that Arthur's head hadn't moved, that he hadn't shouted and sounded the alarms, Myasako jumped behind the curtains just as Martin's mother and Jacobson entered the room.

"This is Arthur," Jacobson said as they walked past his bed. "He's not feeling very friendly tonight."

Arthur was still staring up at the ceiling, as if he was on very strong painkillers.

"How many of those tablets did you give him?" Jacobson asked the nurse who walked in.

"Sir, I'm so sorry. I just gave him one, but he somehow...I don't know how...but he managed to take the bottle from me when I wasn't looking. He took an extra two, and I think that's why he's...unresponsive."

Jacobson approached his son and looked down at his face.

"Arthur! Arthur! Is he alive? Is he Ok?"

"Yes, yes," the nurse said. She was Chinese, and she was looking at the boy on the bed. "Yes, he's fine, he is just very drowsy, that's all."

Jacobson stepped back. "Give him whatever you can to liven him up. I can't believe you would be so careless!" He turned away from her.

"So sorry," the nurse said, and as Myasako looked through a tiny gap in the side of the curtain, he could see that the nurse was smiling.

"Sit, Amanda, please sit," Jacobson said to Martin's mother.

Myasako stood completely still and listened as they talked about boring things – school, subjects, the town, the weather -- all kinds of boring things. But Myasako listened, emptily, as if he had no opinions, until Martin's mother started talking about more important matters.

"So, why is it that Arthur picks on my son at school?" she said.

"Ah, I'm not sure, to be honest," Jacobson said, looking at the table to avoid her eyes. "But I have spoken with him about it. He will certainly not do it anymore."

"But it's been happening for years. You know I have complained to the school but you have never turned up to speak with me. Why only now have you asked me round?"

Jacobson brought his fingers up to his face and rested his chin on his hands.

"Is it because this time Arthur actually got hurt?" she said. "Now you pay attention because *your* son was hurt instead of mine?"

Jacobson sat back. "Perhaps, yes," he said. "Perhaps it took this beating for me to be on the other end, and realise how terrible fighting and bullying is. If that Japanese boy hadn't been bullying Arthur..."

"I'm sorry?" Martin's mother interrupted. "Myasako is not a bully. He..."

"He is a bully. There is direct evidence. He hurt my son very badly..."

"Yes but in self-defence."

"I think not."

"Oh, you know I think I'd like to leave," Martin's mother suddenly said. "I thought this conversation would be reasonable, that you would be reasonable, but for you to suggest and be so blind as to not see that your son is a little monster, then I don't know why we are here."

Jacobson stood as she did.

"I'm sorry, Amanda," he said, raising his hands. "I'm sorry. I'm so very sorry. You're right. I just don't want to admit it. My son is a bully. Yes, he is. Please, sit, the food will be ready soon."

At that moment the waiter brought in the starter. Prawns in a strangely shaped cone dish.

"Will you at least join me for this starter? You're right, again, I'm sorry."

Martin's mother put her handbag down and sat. Then she took her knife and fork, and quietly began to eat. Myasako looked through again and could see Jacobson was not eating. He was staring at her, smiling slightly.

"Now, where is young Myasako?" he said.

"He's at home. He didn't want to come. He had this wild idea about you setting a trap for us, how you were going to do terrible things to us once we came into your home, as revenge for what he did to your son."

"Did he? Did he really?" Jacobson said, leaning back with raised eyebrows. Myasako hid from view completely.

There was a pause.

"How are the prawns?"

"Very nice indeed," Martin's mother said. "Do you always have a chef on call?"

"Yes," Jacobson said. "He's the best."

"Yes, well he..." Myasako heard a knife and fork being dropped.

"What's in this?" Martin's mother suddenly said, sounding alarmed, as if she had just seen something terrible.

"What do you mean?" Jacobson asked.

"I feel...I feel dizzy, like the world is...is mushy and..."

Myasako looked through the tiny gap in front of him and saw Martin's mother fall off her chair and collapse to the floor.

Jacobson stood up.

"She's ready!" he called, and four large men walked in, each taking a limb, an arm or a leg, and they were carrying her limp body out of the room and into another. Jacobson threw his napkin gently on the table and followed after.

Myasako took his nunchuks out of his bag, and he followed. He followed the noise of footsteps, Jacobson's heavily clicking shoes, and he held both nunchuks in one hand, with the other outstretched for silence and balance. He noticed the keys in his pocket started to jingle ever so slightly, and he pressed them down on to his leg with his free hand.

He could see them down the corridor, and suddenly he sensed a nurse walking through to the side of him.

He darted behind a statue of a lion and the nurse walked past. He heard her muttering to herself:

"Now he is a good boy. Give him a few more pills, and now he is a good boy." She kept walking, in private dialogue with herself, and Myasako moved again down the grand corridor with fine paintings and golden trims on the walls, and he saw the men, Amanda and Jacobson turn down a corner at the end of the house, and begin to walk down some steps.

More staff were walking through in between rooms. At one point there was a statue of a Samurai standing at the wall. Myasako had to freeze and blend with it as two male housekeepers walked past, in conversation with each other about white bed sheets. Myasako kept walking, and he approached the stairs.

He started floating down the staircase that began to wind and spiral, and after what felt like minutes of walking, he was at the bottom, in a cold, dark and enormous basement, where Martin's mother was being strapped to a bed, and the men were preparing injection needles.

Martin's mother began to stir and wake up.

Suddenly she started to scream. One of the large men put his hands on her mouth, muffling the awful sound, and eventually she stopped screaming.

"Now, here is what is going to happen," Jacobson said to her, walking around, clicking his shoes on the hard floor, and staring up at the ceiling.

"You will take me to Myasako. You will take me to your home, and I will be accompanied by these men. They are trained killers. You will let me in your home, compliantly, and you will let me take Myasako away. After that, you will never hear from me again, and I promise you that Arthur will never lay a hand on your son. How does that sound?"

Martin's mother was trembling.

"Give her the first injection," Jacobson ordered. "This is to make you compliant. You will be like a different woman after a dose of this..."

One of the men picked up a syringe full of green liquid, and he began to attach a long needle to it.

"Wait. Why do you want Myasako?" she asked, her mouth still slightly muffled by a man's hand.

"To correct what he did to my son," Jacobson said.

"Well why not just take him when you had the chance at my house?"

"It was too risky to be seen stealing a child from a home. My relationship with the chief of police is still not strong enough to survive that. I thought it would be much easier for you to just bring him here for us to capture in private. Since he did not come, since you did not listen to the boy and still came alone, my backup plan is to have you as the guardian, legally hand him over to me. There will be no scene, no illegal activity, nothing to worry about."

"I'll never hand him over, even with all that green stuff inside of me," Martin's mother said, and she spat at Jacobson but Jacobson was too far away to reach.

"Dose her," Jacobson said. "And before you do..." Suddenly Jacobson was hit, and he was on the floor. One end of a nunchuk had flown across the side of his head, and he now lay crumpled on the ground.

"What was that?" one of the men said. It was dark and dim in the basement, only the bed and the syringes were well lit.

The man holding the syringe of green fluid went down next, as if he had been touched by death, and as he fell his body landed on the needle and syringe, and the green liquid was pumped into his body.

"There's someone in here!" one of the other men shouted, and soon his leg was struck and he dropped to the ground and his head was struck straight after.

"Run!" one of the other men said, and as he ran he was tripped, and he hit his head on the hard floor as he fell.

Only one man was left, he couldn't see anyone around him. It was too dark. Jacobson always liked to do his dark deeds in low light, and had always refused to have the room brightly lit like a laboratory. Then the one remaining man heard a voice come from behind him.

"You will unstrap her, and you will escort us out of this building, and out of this property."

The man panicked and swung his fist behind him. Myasako ducked and struck back at the man's throat, and the man was soon on the floor gasping for air.

"Come on, we have to go," Myasako said, unstrapping Martin's mother's arms and legs from the bed.

"Myasako I'm sorry! I'm so sorry I didn't believe you."

"Just come. Let's go," he said, and he left three men unconscious, one clinging for air, and he remembered his father's voice:

"Compassionately incapacitate all enemies. Even one breath of an adversary can lead to the exposure of the ninja."

Myasako turned to the one remaining man who was still conscious, and he choked him just like he did the security officer, until he too was asleep.

"Take off your shoes," he said to Martin's mother. "They are too loud."

"Ok," she said, taking off her heels and running with him to the stairs.

"Let's go," he said, silently running upwards, with her behind him, making shuffling, grating noises on the stairs every time she stepped.

"Silently," Myasako whispered gently, and eventually she was being so loud that he asked her to jump on to his back. She jumped on and Myasako was unmoved, strong like a bull and still silent as he treaded so lightly that Martin's mother could only hear her own breathing.

He glided up the stairs and soon they were at the top, close to an exit.

Myasako was peering around the corner, looking for staff. Then he darted out into the light and ran towards a large double door made of fine oak.

He grabbed the handle but it was locked. He quickly pulled his keys from his pocket that he had taken from the security guard, and started to try them. None of them were working, and he couldn't stand in plain site by the door for too long.

He darted again off to the side behind a large plant and put Martin's mother down. He was stuck. Staff were walking around everywhere and he didn't know what to do. There were no windows around. None of his keys had worked.

Myasako got his nunchuks, reached out quickly and struck the door with them three times, as if the door was being knocked.

"Myasako!" Martin's mother hissed. She was hiding behind the tall plant. "What are you doing?"

"Knocking," he said. He knocked louder, as loud as he could, and soon a young member of the kitchen staff was running through the corridor, coming to open the door.

"I'm coming!" he said. Myasako did not realise this was the staff entrance.

The young man had a key, put it in the door and opened it. He stared out into the night. No one was there. He stepped outside, walked a few paces forward, and looked around.

"Geoff? Geoff are you here? You're late. Is this a joke?"

The young man heard something. He turned around and saw a shadow move outside the house on the wall.

"Geoff? Don't mess about, Geoff."

The young man walked back towards the door and stared at the thicket of bushes surrounding the path that went around the house.

"Geoff, I'm locking this door again if you don't show yourself."

He waited.

"Fine, you can stay out here, but I doubt you will get paid!" And the young man stormed inside, closed the door behind him, and noticed that there was some soil on the floor, some soil that seemed to have fallen out from the large plant pot standing on the table beside him.

The soil was in a strange place, too far from the plant to have just fallen if adjusted.

He stared, swept it up with his hands, put the soil back in the pot and called one of the maids to mop the area.

Myasako and Amanda were running across the lawn again, to the front gate where the security office was. The gate was closed, and Myasako took the keys out of his pocket and opened the office door. The security guard was awake but still tied up.

"You little rotter! How dare you do that to me! I'll make sure you never see the light of day for this! What's your name?"

Myasako found a button, a large green button with "Gate" written on it. He pushed it, and the gates began to open.

"Thank you for this," Myasako said, and he gave the office keys back to the man, left him tied up, and left the man's mobile phone and walkie-talkie still out of reach.

Myasako bowed, ran out of the room, closed the door behind him, and together with Martin's mother, they escaped the Muldridge residence.

勇
気

Courage

Courage is not the absence of fear,
but the ability to act in spite of it.

Chapter 11 - The Aftermath

When they were back home, Martin's mother's mind was racing.

"How did you manage all of that?" she said. "Weren't you afraid?"

"Of course," Myasako said.

"So how could you do it? How could you risk yourself like that?"

"I knew it was right for me to do it. If you know something is right, then I am taught that the fear is not a bad thing. If we embrace the fear, and then attack the task that we are afraid of, then we will prosper."

"Well, thank you Myasako. I think I owe you my life."

"You are welcome," he said, bowing. "It is not safe for either of us for me to stay here any longer. He wants to get to me by using you. I must leave soon and go back to Japan. I must leave tomorrow."

"Ok," Martin's mother said. "But before you go, could you teach me a few things?"

*

The next morning, Myasako was training Martin's mother. He showed her kicks, punches, arm locks, throws, and how to move silently without effort.

"Sometimes to do things effortlessly takes a lot of effort beforehand," he said. "I can show you what to practice, but you're the one who has to make sure you practice."

"Maybe I should go to a class, a self-defence class or something as well," Martin's mother said, realising she wanted to be able to fight anyone if she had to.

"Yes, good idea, just make sure it is as realistic as possible," Myasako said. "Sometimes people in Japan act as if they are ninjas, but they are nothing of the sort. Make sure no one fools you into giving you a false sense of security by doing drills that will never work in real life. Now, we end our session with meditation."

"Oh, no," Martin's mother said. "No don't worry about that, Myasako, I can't meditate properly. I can never turn my mind off."

"Then that is why you *should* meditate," Myasako said, sitting down on the garage floor. "And anyway, it is not about turning your mind off, it is about being at peace with your mind, and allowing it to calm down by itself. Come on, I have to leave soon."

With twenty minutes before Myasako had to leave, Amanda pulled up a chair beside him, sat on it, and closed her eyes.

*

In Japan the next morning, Kuyasaki was waiting for Martin to walk in to the dojo. It was early in the morning.

"Are we running today?" Martin asked, bowing as he walked in.

"No. It is not safe," Kuyasaki said. "I have to go and see my brother. I have to stop him from wanting to destroy me and my family."

"How?" Martin said, coming in to sit down.

"I'm not sure yet. An answer is not clear. He will refuse to sit with me peacefully. If I ask him, he will become even more alert to my arrival. I feel stealth may be my best option, to sneak into his compound and find him alone."

"Well when? Can I come?"

"No, it is not safe. I feel your stay here is no longer a fair one. You might be in danger. When my brother finds out what has happened, he might send more men directly here, and there will be a fight. We have to send you home."

"No! If there's a fight I want to help!" Martin said.

"Myasako is coming home soon. He came to me in a dream last night and he told me he wasn't safe. He said that there was a man after him, and he was endangering your mother by being there."

"What? What's happened?" Martin felt jumpy and fiery all of a sudden.

"I'm not sure. But he said the issue might not be resolved. There may be challenges that you need to face when back home, people you have to deal with and stay away from. I'm not sure what all of this means."

"Don't you have a phone? I want to call my mum."

"No, I don't, but I told Myasako in my dream that I was sending you back."

"Well how do you know any of that was real?" Martin said, hoping his mother was Ok. "I have dreams all the time that aren't real. Once I was riding on the back of a dinosaur going through space and..."

"Martin," Kuyasaki said. "It is time for you to leave.

"Takashi will protect you as you travel to the airport. Pack your things and prepare to leave. I have arranged you a flight home."

"How?"

"One of the airline employees lives not far from here. I arranged it with her."

"Ok. Ok I'll get ready then," Martin said, wanting to go home and make sure his mother was alright. "Thank you for teaching me, I wish I could have learnt more."

Kuyasaki stood up.

"You have learnt the perfect amount. Your resistance to discipline has been eased, and your openness to practice has been developed. Take those skills home with you, and find a good teacher."

"Thank you," Martin said again, bowing at Kuyasaki, and Kuyasaki bowed back.

"And Martin," Kuyasaki said before the boy turned and walked away. "I have something for you. Here."

Kuyasaki took out a shiny grey stone, and he handed it to Martin. Martin saw that as he took it, the stone flashed with white in the middle.

"What is it?"

"It's protection."

"What? What do I do, throw it at someone?"

"No," Kuyasaki said. "It is an ancient stone that blends with the owner's energy and acts to protect them in times of need. I will not say what it can do, because you will not believe me. There are not many stones like this in the world that I know of. Not even my son has one, because I have taught him to be his own defence. But I feel that for you, if you are facing danger back at home, you may well need it. Keep it until you become your own fortress, and pass it on to someone else who might need it. It will continue to teach you the ways of the ninja, if you listen to it."

Martin looked down at the cold, unmoving stone, and he put it in his pocket.

"Thank you," he said. "I'll look after it."

"No, it will look after you," Kuyasaki said.

*

The flights home for both boys were silent. Both were eager to get back home, where they belonged, to be with those they loved most.

"Martin!" his mother cried as she ran to him at the airport.

"Mum, I'm sorry," he said.

"For what, dear?" she said, wiping a tear from her face.

"I'm sorry for never appreciating you. I'm sorry for never noticing how much you do for me. I'm sorry for never noticing how well you take care of me, how hard you work for me, and I'm sorry for wanting to get away."

She hugged him again.

"That's Ok, dear. Did you enjoy your time away?"

"Yes," he said. "I learnt a lot. Now what's been going on? Are you Ok?"

*

When Myasako returned home, his father was training in the dojo. Myasako approached the entrance, bowed and waited for his father to finish his set of kicks.

"Son," Kuyasaki said, bowing.

"Father," Myasako bowed again. "Father I have an apology to make. All of the training you have had me do, all the relentless discipline and training has not been for nothing. I see now what you have turned me in to, how well I am able to defend myself and help others in the world. I see now what you were doing, and I'm grateful."

Kuyasaki smiled and looked at his son.

"You are welcome," he replied. "I also see that my obsession with your greatness sometimes means I do not allow you to enjoy your life. I am now more open to leisure time, it is more important than I have realised, and without it, a man's training suffers. Now please, enter the dojo, I want to discuss what has been happening with your Uncle Senzi."

Myasako entered the dojo, smelt the familiar smell of the mats and the stillness, and he realised he was home again.

Love

*With love at the heart of all actions,
success is inevitable.*

終わり

The End

Endings are nothing but
opportunities for new beginnings...

Continue The Adventure!

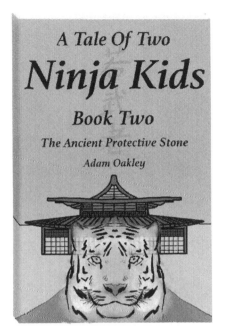

Find out what happens when Myasako teams up with his father to fight the threat of his evil uncle, and Martin discovers what really happens when the protective stone from Kuyasaki senses danger...

Book 2 available now on Amazon.

Get the full 6-book series on Amazon now, and join the adventures of Martin, Myasako, and a powerful ninja kid named Nayla...

Out Now On Amazon:

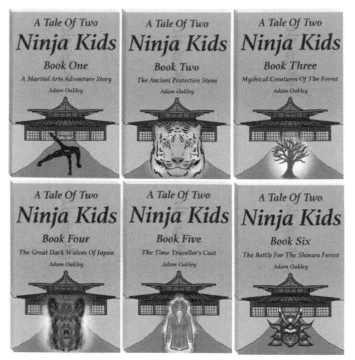

A Tale Of Two
Ninja Kids
Book One
A Martial Arts Adventure Story
Adam Oakley

A Tale Of Two
Ninja Kids
Book Two
The Ancient Protective Stone
Adam Oakley

A Tale Of Two
Ninja Kids
Book Three
Mythical Creatures Of The Forest
Adam Oakley

A Tale Of Two
Ninja Kids
Book Four
The Great Dark Wolves Of Japan
Adam Oakley

A Tale Of Two
Ninja Kids
Book Five
The Time Traveller's Coat
Adam Oakley

A Tale Of Two
Ninja Kids
Book Six
The Battle For The Shinwa Forest
Adam Oakley

Coming Soon:

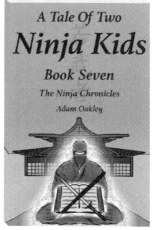

A Tale Of Two
Ninja Kids
Book Seven
The Ninja Chronicles
Adam Oakley

Also By Adam For Ages 8+

Fred: The Creature Sent To Save Us All

Happiness Is Inside: 25 Inspirational Stories For Greater Peace Of Mind

Mythical Creatures Of The Forest

*If you enjoyed this book, **please leave a review on Amazon** – it helps the book to reach more people!*

Thank you.

Follow Adam on social media here:

@ninjakidsbook

@adamoakleybooks

About The Author

Adam is not yet a fully-fledged ninja with skills to rival Myasako's, but maybe one day he will be.

For now he is happy doing kickboxing, wrestling and Brazilian jiu jitsu during the week, in between growing organic food, writing, and spending time with his family.

He hopes you loved reading the book, and he is grateful for any young readers or parents who can leave a review on Amazon to help the book reach more people.

He thanks you for your support, and is always available to contact via one of his websites:

www.AdamOakleyBooks.com

www.InnerPeaceNow.com

Manufactured by Amazon.ca
Bolton, ON